In a Garden

For Sophie, who is caring and curious
—T. M.

For Hudson, my creature seeker and forever gardener
—A. S.

SIMON & SCHUSTER BOOKS FOR YOUNG READERS
An imprint of Simon & Schuster Children's Publishing Division
1230 Avenue of the Americas, New York, New York 10020
Text copyright © 2020 by Tim McCanna
Illustrations copyright © 2020 by Aimée Sicuro
SIMON & SCHUSTER BOOKS FOR YOUNG READERS is a trademark of Simon & Schuster, Inc.
For information about special discounts for bulk purchases, please contact Simon & Schuster Special Sales
at 1-866-506-1949 or business@simonandschuster.com.
The Simon & Schuster Speakers Bureau can bring authors to your live event. For more information or to book an event,
contact the Simon & Schuster Speakers Bureau at 1-866-248-3049 or visit our website at www.simonspeakers.com.
Book design by Laurent Linn
The text for this book was set in Mercurius CT Std.
The illustrations for this book were rendered in watercolor, ink, charcoal, and Photoshop.
Manufactured in China
0823 SCP
4 6 8 10 9 7 5
Library of Congress Cataloging-in-Publication Data
Names: McCanna, Tim, author. | Sicuro, Aimée, 1976– illustrator.
Title: In a garden / Tim McCanna ; illustrated by Aimée Sicuro.
Description: First edition. | New York : Simon & Schuster Books for Young Readers, [2020] | "A Paula Wiseman Book."
Identifiers: LCCN 2019006399| ISBN 9781534417977 (hardcover) | ISBN 9781534417984 (eBook)
Subjects: | CYAC: Stories in rhyme. | Gardens—Fiction. | Garden ecology—Fiction.
Classification: LCC PZ8.3.M13193 In 2020 | DDC [E]—dc23
LC record available at https://lccn.loc.gov/2019006399

In a Garden

Written by
Tim McCanna

Illustrated by
Aimée Sicuro

A Paula Wiseman Book
Simon & Schuster Books for Young Readers
New York London Toronto Sydney New Delhi

In a garden
on a hill
sparrows chirp
and crickets trill.

In the earth
a single seed
sits beside a millipede.

Worms and termites
dig and toil
moving through the garden soil.

Then at last
a tiny shoot
ever slowly
forms a root.

First a seedling
then a sprout
pushing
bursting
up and out.

*In a garden
day by day
newborn flowers
find their way.*

Sunlight warms the morning air.
Dewdrops shimmer
here and there.

Earwigs scuttle.
Beetles scurry.
Roly-polies
scoot and worry.

Sleepy slugs
and garden snails
leave behind their silver trails.

Frantic teams of busy ants
scramble up the stems of plants.

In a garden
week by week
little creatures
hunt and squeak.

All the while
a sprout is growing
without anybody knowing.

Buds emerge and leaves unfold
braving wind
and heat and cold.

CARROTS

PEPPERS

LETTUCE

Stretching, spreading
open wide—
just the perfect place to hide.

Underneath, it's safe and snug
for a lonely ladybug.

In a garden
showers fall,
dainty drinks
for one and all.

Flower petals
bold and bright
blossom in the beaming light.

Blooms of every shape and size
call to bees and butterflies.

Daisy, foxglove,
tulip, plum,
daffodil,
chrysanthemum.

Sips of nectar
warm and sweet.
Pollen clings to heads and feet.

Round and round
they buzz and flit,
only pause to rest a bit.

In a garden
bugs aglow
flashing, flying
to and fro.

Lacewings, gnats,
mosquitos, spiders,
dragonflies, and water striders
live among the cattail reeds,
lily pads, and waterweeds

keeping hid from hungry eyes
using colors to disguise.

Crafty bugs with clever tricks
look like leaves
or bark
or sticks.

In a garden
full of green
many moments
go unseen.

Finding shelter
in the shade
careful rows of eggs are laid
as a cool and gentle breeze
whispers through the tops of trees.

Then a seed
slips to the ground
sinking in
without a sound.

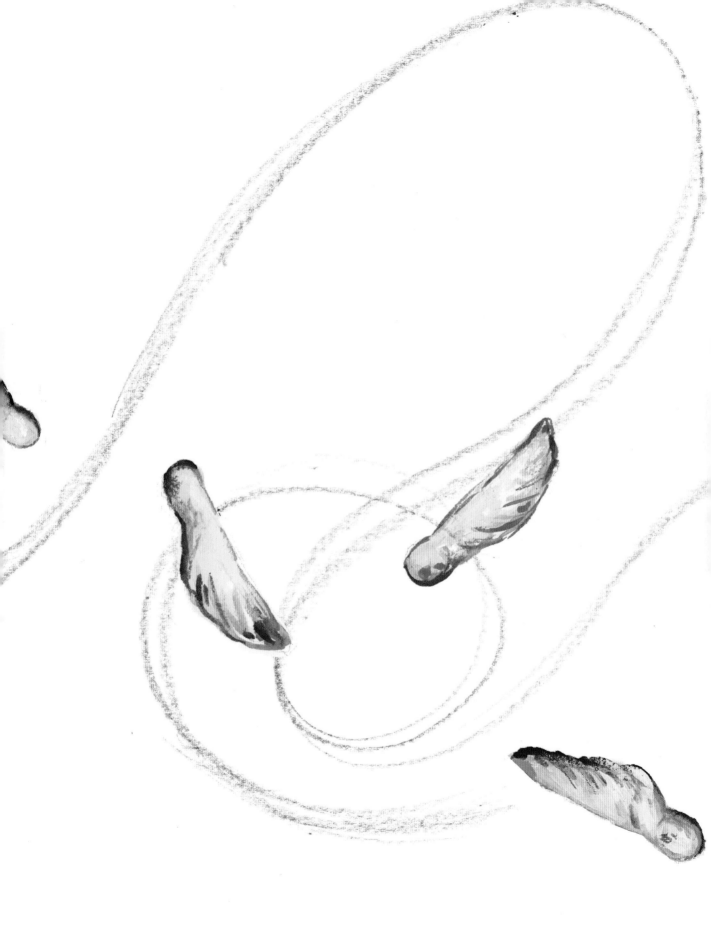

Time goes by
and by
and then . . .

life returns
to start
again.

Always changing
never still
in a garden
on a hill.

HOW DOES A GARDEN GROW?

Gardens are filled with a variety of life. Plants, bugs, birds, mice, snakes, and many other organisms come and go in a garden ecosystem. Throughout the seasons of a year, plants grow, flourish, die, and start the process over and over again, thanks in part to the roles living creatures—especially insects—play in a garden.

For millions of years, plants and bugs have evolved together. They have a symbiotic relationship, which means they have adapted to help each other live and grow. For instance, for a seed in the ground to germinate, or start growing, it needs water, oxygen, and nutrient-rich soil. Earthworms and millipedes eat decomposing plants and spread a natural fertilizer for growing plants to use. Through their digging and tunneling, earthworms improve the soil. Their movement helps soil absorb nutrients, provides aeration, and helps prevent the soil from eroding.

Many bugs live in and around the leaves and stems of plants and flowers. Insects such as beetles, lacewings, and ladybugs eat tiny mites and aphids, which are harmful to plants. Praying mantises hunt and eat larger pests such as grasshoppers, flies, and crickets. In return, the plants provide fruit and nectar, shade and shelter from the weather, and camouflage, which helps insects hide from predators.

Bees, moths, and butterflies are attracted to the colors and smells of certain flowers. Some insects have evolved extra long tongues and legs to reach down into their favorite flowers and drink up a sugary water called nectar. Flying insects move from bloom to bloom, collecting and distributing pollen, which promotes plant reproduction. That way, flowers can grow new seeds, which will fall to the ground and start again after the old ones die. Meanwhile, bees store nectar in a special stomach and fly it back to their hives so they can make honey.

Humans have been gardening since prehistoric times. The very first forest gardens were created to support beneficial plants and eliminate unwanted species. Earliest records of gardening can be found in Egyptian tomb paintings from around 1500 BCE. Gardens were popular in ancient Rome, and by the Middle Ages, gardens were used to grow herbs for medicinal purposes. Today, many people grow ornamental gardens around their homes, as well as fruit and vegetable gardens. Most major cities have large botanical gardens and public vegetable gardens where anyone can tend a small patch of soil. Whatever their purpose, size, or location, gardens bring life, beauty, and harmony to the world around us.